Thistle's First Hoof Trim

Lady Thistle, the Horse
BOOK FIVE

D.H. ANDERSON
Illustrations by STEVEN LESTER

Thistle's First Hoof Trim

Paperback ISBN 978-1-960007-58-2
HardBack ISBN 978-1-960007-57-5
eBOOK ISBN 978-1-960007-59-9

Published by
Little Blessing Books
an imprint of
Orison Publishers, Inc.
PO Box 188, Grantham, PA 17027
www.OrisonPublishers.com

Acknowledgments

Contributing Veterinarian: Apryle Horbal, VMD

Thistle and Her Mom, Polly

Lady Thistle

A young horse, whose lively spirit inspired the writing of her real life story. Through her distinctive personality and her talent for connecting with her family and friends, she provided the emotional and illustrative components for this book series.

Thank You!

A special thank you to David P. Bentrem,
Certified Journeyman Farrier (AFA CJF) for his
continued care of our horses over the years as well as
his professional input into *Thistle's First Hoof Trim*.

Lady Thistle is three months old. She still drinks her mother's milk, even though she enjoys hay and the delicious green grass in the pasture. She is growing fast—her legs are long and lanky. Thistle wants to be just like the big horses now, but so many things they do are scary!

It is July, and the summer sun is bright and hot. The older horses stay in the barn during the day and go out at night when it's cooler. Thistle would like to go outdoors in the evening, but Polly says, "No, you're too young to go out at night. It's hard to see in the dark."

Instead Thistle and her mom go out for a few hours each morning. Shade trees and a run-in allow them to escape the hot sun.

Summer brings flies, which bother the horses. Dr. Apryle visits the barn and talks to the farmhands about fly masks and a special spray that protects horses from flies.

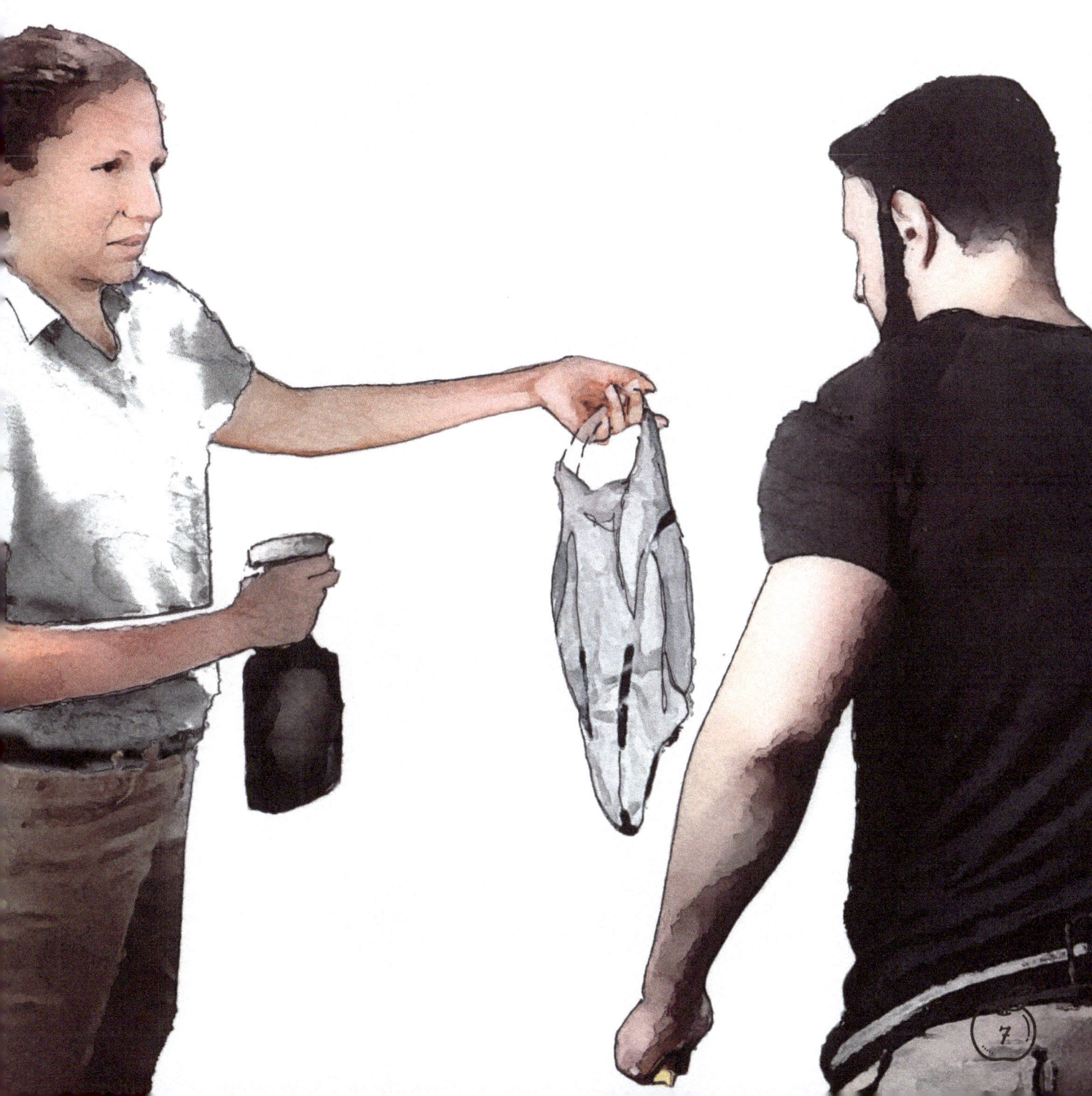

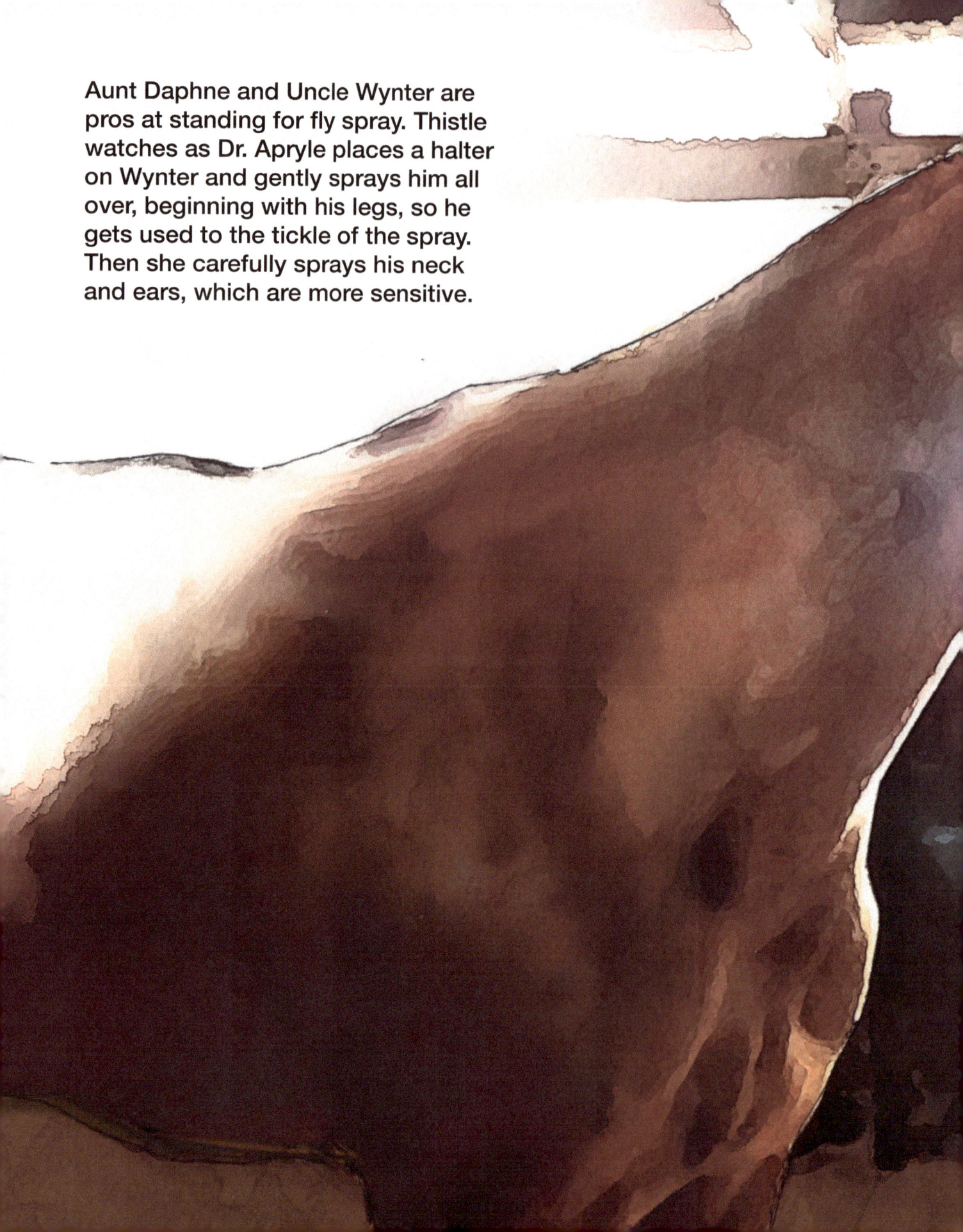

Aunt Daphne and Uncle Wynter are pros at standing for fly spray. Thistle watches as Dr. Apryle places a halter on Wynter and gently sprays him all over, beginning with his legs, so he gets used to the tickle of the spray. Then she carefully sprays his neck and ears, which are more sensitive.

Thistle and Polly are nervous when Apryle enters their stall, carrying the spray bottle. Polly moves toward the back of the stall watching Dr. Apryle and trying not to be scared. Thistle hides behind her mom.

Apryle comforts Polly, and Polly wiggles just a bit as she is sprayed. Polly raises her head to get away from the fly mask, but with gentle pressure on her halter, Apryle slips the mask on.

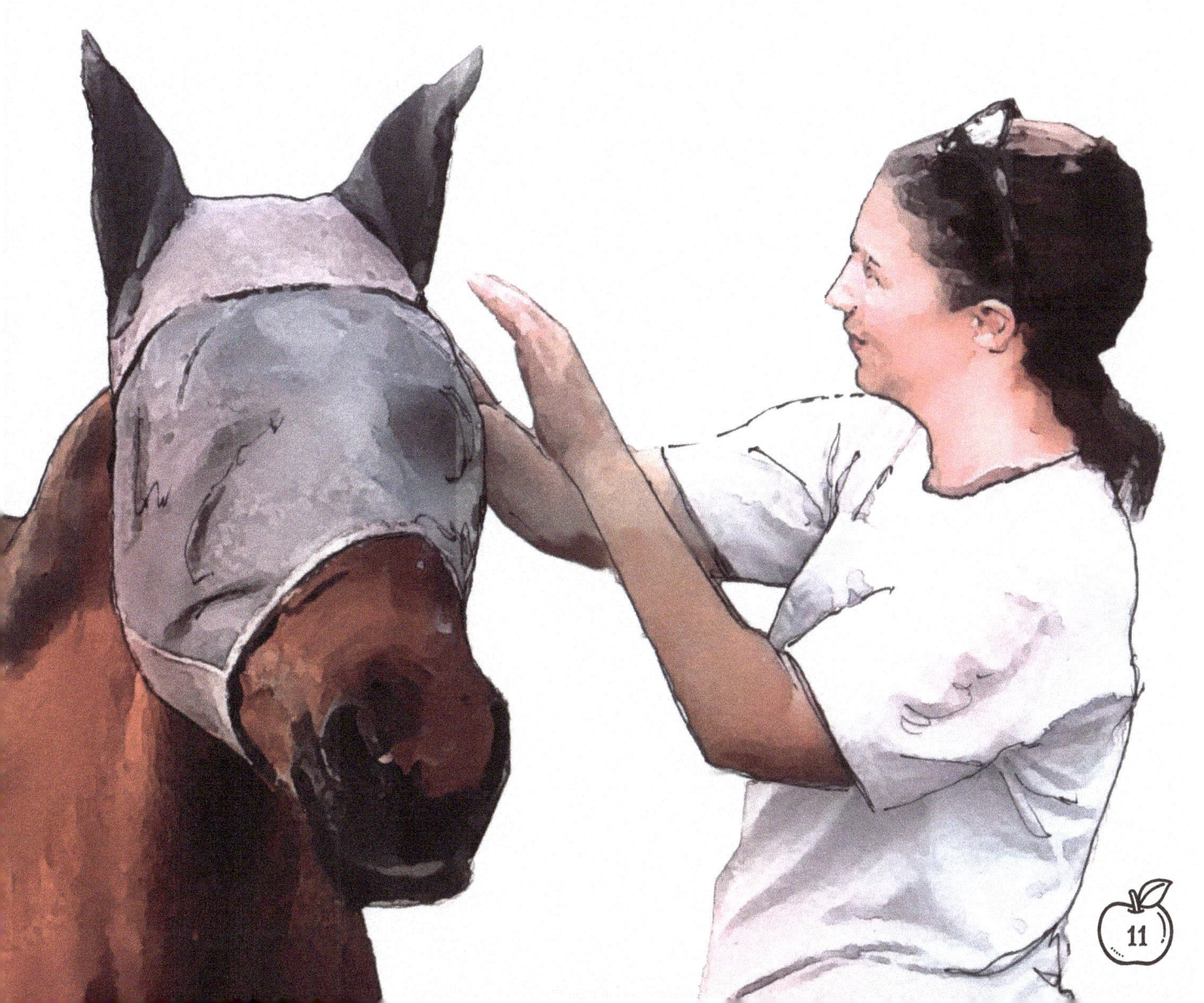

Thistle is curious, but she is also frightened. She trusts Dr. Apryle, who treated the cut on her leg when she was younger. But now her eyes grow wide when Dr. Apryle takes hold of her halter and lightly sprays her legs. "Good girl," the veterinarian says. "That's enough spray for today."

Then she lets Thistle sniff a fly mask. Thistle decides she will wear the mask, just like Mom! She feels like a big horse as she heads out to the pasture.

But Thistle's lessons are not finished yet!

David, the farrier, has been coming to Waterdam Farm for many years. He cares for horses' feet by trimming hooves and putting shoes on horses that are used for working and riding. He and Dr. Apryle know it is time for Thistle to be checked.

Thistle passes Farrier David's truck as she walks to the barn.
She sees Yanik playing with David's dog, Red.

16

The farrier greets the big horses by name; they nicker in response.
David slowly reaches out and calms a worried Thistle.

17

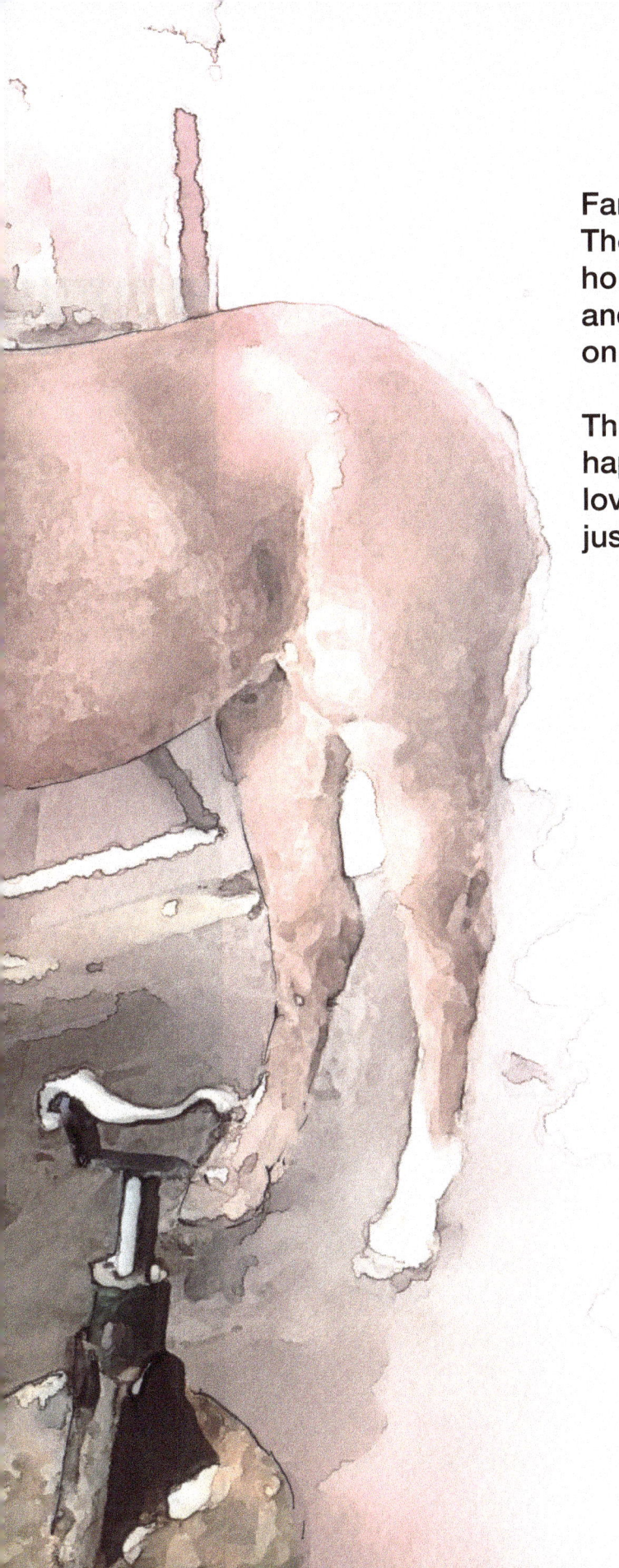

Farrier David brings in his equipment.
There is a hoof stand with a strap to
hold a horse's foot up off the floor
and a set of tools and nails in a caddy
on wheels.

Thistle knows something different is
happening, and she is worried. She
loves to make new friends, but she is
just not sure about this man

Thistle watches as Daphne goes first. The farrier checks each hoof for problems. Then he places one of Daphne's front feet on the stand and pulls off her old shoe with his pull-off tool. He uses his nippers to trim her hoof to the correct length. He smooths the edges and files down thick places with a metal rasp.

Finally, David lifts her foot and holds the shoe in place. Then he hammers nails through the shoe and into the hoof.

David knows exactly where to place the nails, so this does not hurt Daphne.

Rasp

Nippers

Hoof Knife

HOOF BOTTOM VIEW

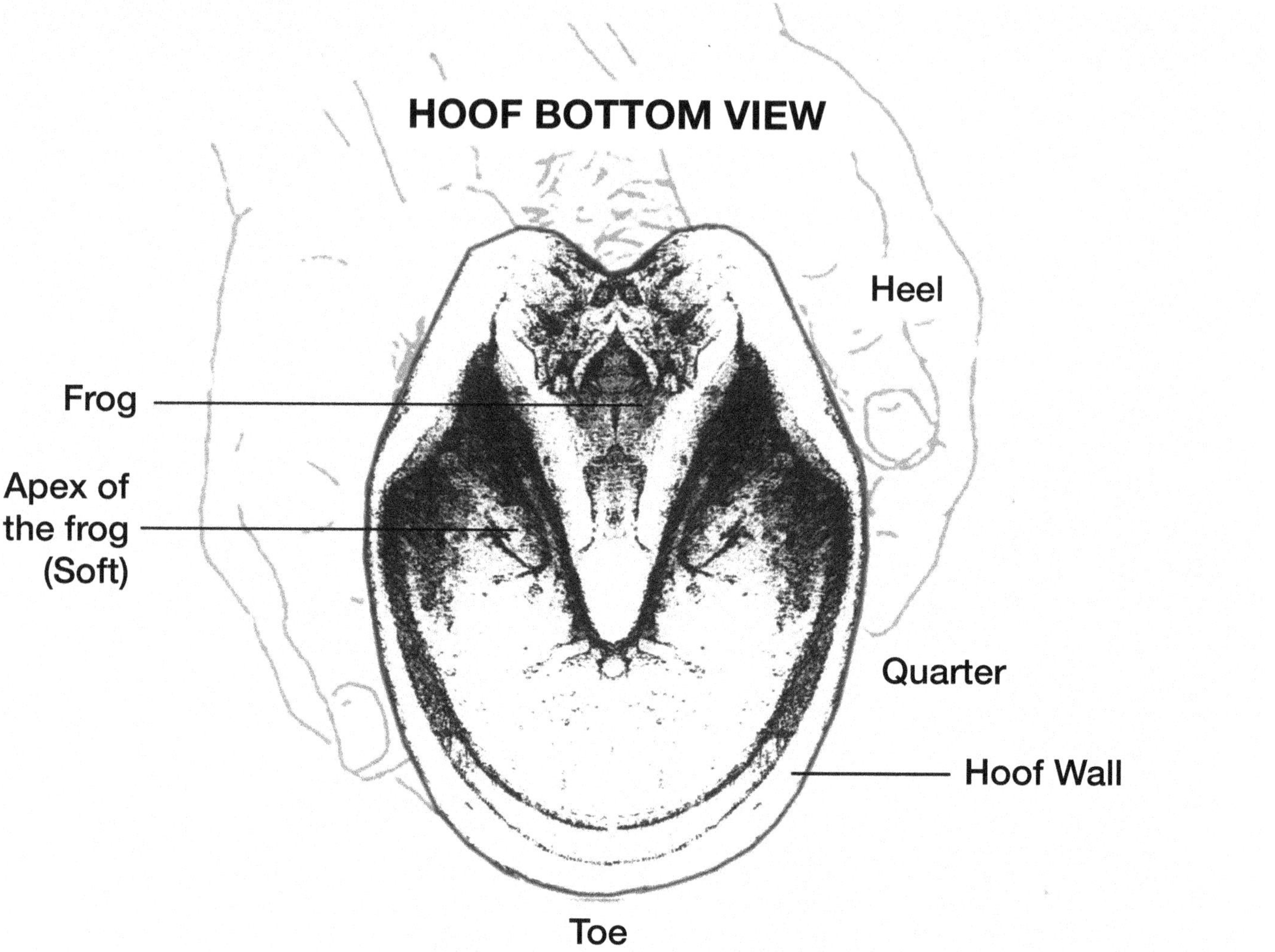

Heel

Frog

Apex of
the frog
(Soft)

Quarter

Hoof Wall

Toe

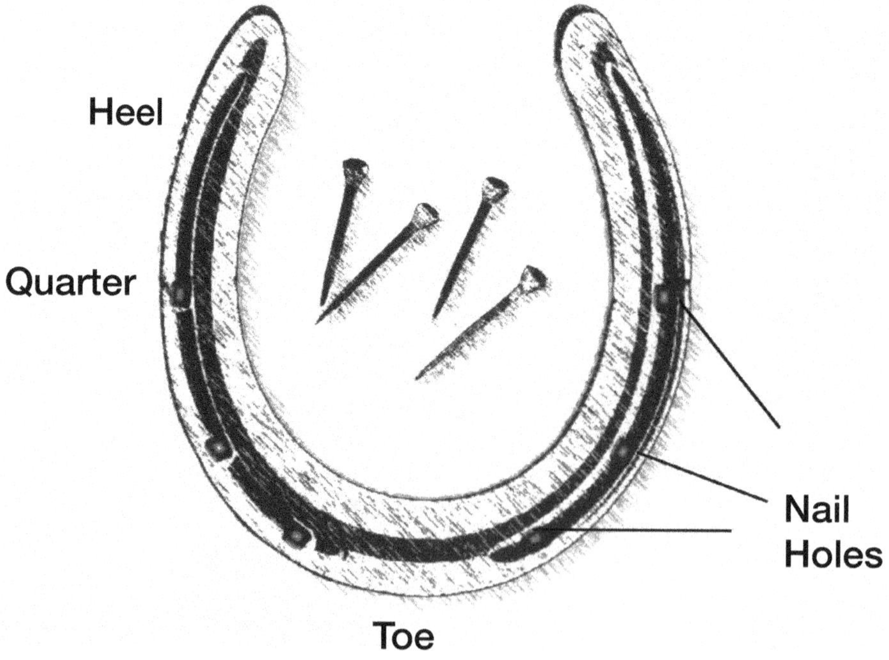

Heel

Quarter

Nail
Holes

Toe

SHOE and NAILS

Some horses wear shoes and some do not, depending on their job.

LATERAL

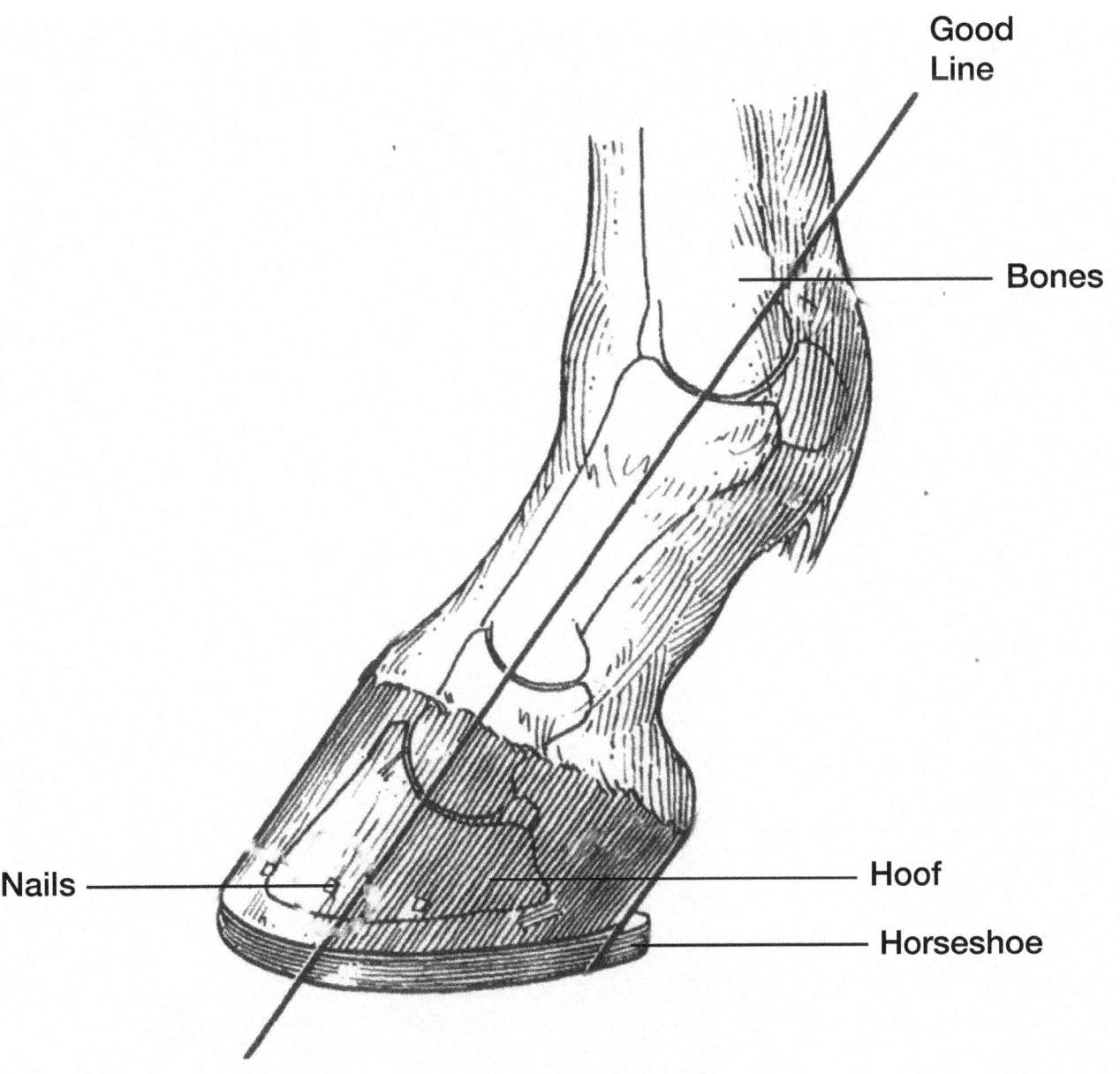

Good Line

Bones

Nails

Hoof

Horseshoe

David enters Polly's stall with his tools and gently asks her to move back. Thistle wants to get away from him; she does not want *anything* nailed to her feet! But she also wants to stay with Mom.

David tickles Polly's leg, asking her to lift her foot. She does not wear shoes, but he checks the foot, trims and files the hoof, and gently places it down.

"This is safe," Polly nickers to Thistle. "It's part of being a grown-up horse."

"But it might hurt!" Thistle says with her frightened eyes.

David places Thistle's halter on and lets her choose where to stand. Thistle stands right next to Polly. He slowly bends down, picks up a front foot, and gets his nippers out of his pocket. Thistle pulls away, but David gently rubs her leg, and suddenly her trimming is underway. It doesn't hurt!

She lets the farrier trim all four hooves. Then she pokes her head out of the stall to let everyone know how grown-up she is!

This was a stressful but exciting day for young Lady Thistle. The farmhands serve the horses' evening grain and place fresh hay in their stalls. Thistle falls sound asleep and dreams of being a grown-up horse. Will she be a racehorse? A show horse? Soon, she will know.

At dusk, the barn is checked, and all is quiet but for the sound of continuous munching of hay.

Did You Know...?

Pesky insects like flies attack horses' moist eyes and noses. They bite the insides of the ears, causing bleeding. When flies bite their legs, horses stomp their feet, which can damage their hooves.

Fly masks are a barrier against bugs, dirt, and wind, and they offer sun protection for horses' eyes and noses. But it is a challenge to find a mask that a horse will accept. Some horses try to remove their masks and will even help other horses do so. A lightweight "sheet" and "boots" can cover the entire body of the horse.

Various sprays also help to keep the flies and other bugs away. Different sprays must be tried to find the one that best protects against the specific pests in various fields.

A **farrier** is a skilled professional in **equine** (horse) care, including the trimming and balancing of horse hooves and the placing of shoes, If needed. The farrier also helps the veterinarian diagnose and treat any hoof-related problems. The farrier and veterinarian know all about horse **anatomy** (body parts) and **physiology** (how the parts work together).

A horse may not need shoes if it is not being ridden or worked. Horses need shoes when being ridden for Dressage, Western pleasure, Reigning, Cross-country, Racing, Cart trotting, Jumping, Other sporting and recreational disciplines

Horses also need shoes for walking on hard, rocky surfaces; doing farmwork; or pulling carriages. A "hospital plate" is used to cover an entire hoof when an injury needs to heal. A reigning horse needs special plates for sliding.

The farrier must choose the correct type of shoe and adapt it for the best fit. Farrier David sometimes uses the **anvil** on the back of his truck to pound the shoe and shape it to fit the foot.

Polly and the Birth Day

D.H. ANDERSON
Illustrations by STEVEN LESTER

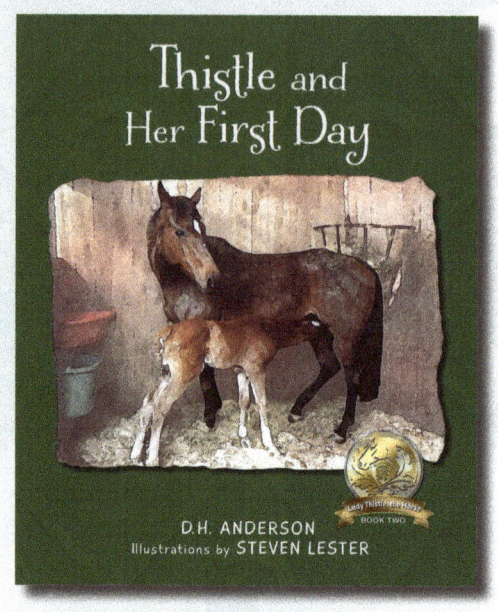

Thistle and Her First Day

D.H. ANDERSON
Illustrations by STEVEN LESTER

Thistle Starts Exploring

D.H. ANDERSON
Illustrations by STEVEN LESTER

Thistle Gets Hurt

D.H. ANDERSON
Illustrations by STEVEN LESTER

Watch for Lady Thistle's Journey to continue.

SCAN ME